Principle Woods™ Celebrates Courage

Author
Sandra Stroner Sivulich

Illustrator
Kevin Shore

Principle Woods, Inc.
One San Jose Place, Suite 11
Jacksonville, Florida 32257
www.principlewoods.com

Designed by David Whitlock, Principle Design Group, Inc.

0502-02ED
ISBN 0-9700601-9-X

This book belongs to

_____

Dedicated to my father, Frank. J. Stroner,
who shared his love of words with me

Contents

The Monsters Are Coming!

The thunder was loud. The lightning was bright. The rain was heavy and steady. The storm was big.

All the animals who lived in Principle Woods were glad. They were safe and dry in their homes.

But...Springer, the bunny, was afraid of the thunder,

the lightning,

and the rain.

He tried to go to sleep. But he just could not. Every time the thunder would rumble and the lightning would flash, his eyes would open wider and his long ears would hear more than the thunder.

He was sure he was hearing someone trying to get into his burrow.

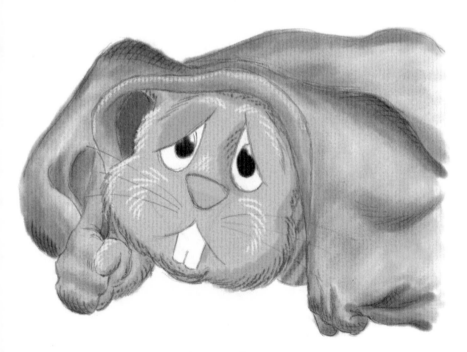

He could hear the scritch-scratching sound over and over again.

He was sure he was hearing an ugly, mean monster with long fingernails trying to dig into his burrow.

He was afraid. He could not move. He did not want to move in case the ugly, mean monster got in and saw him. He hid under his blanket. After a long, long time, he fell asleep.

At the same time at Busy Beaver Creek, Chopsie, the beaver, was listening to the storm. She, too, was afraid.

The thunder was loud. The lightning was bright. The rain was heavy and steady. Each time the lightning flashed, it would light up her room.

In the corner of her room, she was
sure she could see a pile of hissing
monsters.

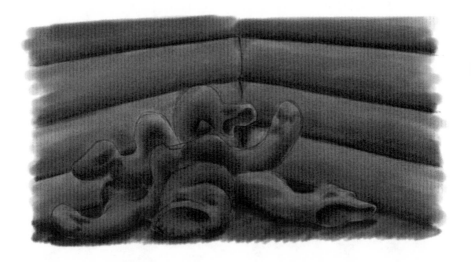

When it was dark, she couldn't see
them, but she knew they were there.

She lay very still under her blankets,
hoping the monsters would not see her.
After a long, long time, she fell asleep.

The next day, the storm was over.
The birds were singing. Springer
jumped out of bed. "Good morning,
Beautiful Day!" he shouted. Then,
he remembered the storm. Next,
he remembered the monster. "Oh,
dear," he thought, "I hope I didn't
wake it up."

Ever so quietly, he tiptoed up to his front door. He listened. No sound. Ever so slowly, he opened his front door, and then he saw it.

There was no monster. There was only a big branch that had fallen from a tree during the storm. The wind had been pushing the branch against the door. The wind and the branch made the scritch-scratching sound.There had been nothing to be afraid of after all!

Meanwhile, at Busy Beaver Creek, the sun was also waking up Chopsie.

"Good morning," she cried out cheerfully.

Then she stopped. She remembered the storm. She remembered the hissing monsters hiding in the corner. Where were the hissing monsters now? All she saw were her dirty clothes piled in the corner.

"Oh," said Chopsie. "How silly of me to think a pile of dirty clothes was a pile of hissing monsters."

Burly, the bear, called all the animals to the clearing with his roar. They needed to see that everyone and everything was all right after the big storm.

The animal friends talked about the storm. Springer told his tale about the scritch-scratching monster. Chopsie told her tale about the hissing monster.

Everyone laughed and cheered when they finished.

Then Sage, the owl, spoke up, "My dear friends, as I fly about Out There, I have learned there are two kinds of dangers. There are REAL dangers, and there are PRETEND dangers. Springer and Chopsie did not know for sure what was making them afraid.

They only knew something sounded strange and scary, and something looked strange and scary. They did the right thing. They stayed away. They had the courage and good sense to wait. They did not rush ahead into a place where they could have gotten hurt. In the morning, when they could see better, they learned the truth and learned they were safe.

Sometimes it is fun to be scared. It is exciting. But real danger is never fun or exciting.

It is very important to understand the difference between REAL danger and PRETEND danger.

Thank you to Springer and Chopsie
for having the courage to share their
tales so we could all learn from them!"

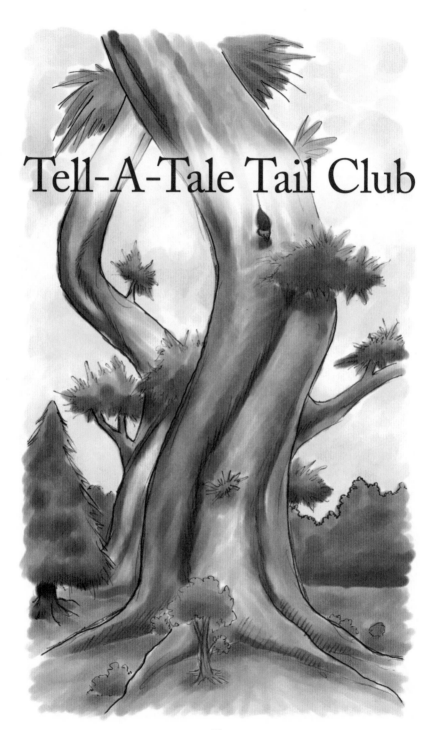

Tell-A-Tale Tail Club

One day, Tipper, the squirrel, had an idea.

He would start a club.

He would be president.

He would be in charge of all the rules.

He would decide who could be in the club.

He would decide who could not be in the club.

He would be very important.

The name of the club would be
Tell-A-Tale Tail Club.

The rules would be:

1) A member must have a tall or
big tail.

2) A member must tell a story or
tale about his tail.

3) Members must talk only to
other members.

Tipper called all his friends.

He told them about the new club.

The friends were very excited.

The friends all wanted to join the club.

The next day all the Principle Woods friends came to Tipper's house, Great Pine. They were ready to start the club.

Tipper called the meeting to order.

"Welcome to the Tell-A-Tale Tail Club.
To start, I will measure all your tails.
Each of you line up and come here
now," ordered Tipper.

Everyone was very happy until
Springer came up to be measured.
His little, fluffy bunny tail was not tall
enough or big enough. Tipper said,
"You cannot be a member of the club.
Your tail is too small. Rules are rules.
Out you go!"

Springer looked at Tipper. Springer looked at all his animal friends. They looked back at him. They did not know what to do. They wanted to be in the club. Tipper had said, "Rules are rules." The rules said that if you are a member, you can only talk to other members.

Springer said, "I cannot help it that my tail is small. This is the only way bunny tails are made.

I did not make it small. You did not make your tail big, either. I am still the same Springer that you all know. Why are you doing this to me? Your club rules make me sad."

Tipper replied, "That's too bad, Springer. Rules are rules. Now, everyone who is in the club, line up."

The animal friends did not know what to do. They did not want to be left out of the club, so they got in line.

"Good," said Tipper. "Springer, you can go home. You are different than we are. You don't belong." The animals were not happy. They were sad about Springer. But, they were glad they could be in the club. They did not want Tipper to tell them, "You are different. You do not belong."

A tiny tear slowly started to run down Springer's face. He turned away from his friends.

Chopsie, the beaver, saw the tear. Chopsie thought about how she would feel if she heard Tipper say, "You are different. You don't belong." Those words hurt others and made them sad.

Chopsie thought about other words that made her friends sad. Chopsie thought about other words that made her friends glad.

"Courage" was one word that made her friends glad. She thought about the word "courage." She thought about how that word could make Springer happy again.

Just saying the word would not work. She must act out the word. It would be hard, but she knew what she had to do.

Instead of following the other animals into Great Pine, she turned around and started to leave.

"Where are you going, Chopsie?" asked Tipper. "The club meeting is over here."

"I know," answered Chopsie, "But I am not going to belong to your club. Your club makes some animals sad. I do not want to belong to such a club. I am going to talk to Springer.

I do not care if his tail is different. What is important is that he is my friend."

Tipper said, "You'll be sorry. The other animals won't talk to you, either. They are in the club. You are not."

Chopsie said, "I do not care. I do not want to be in a club that does not let everyone join."

The other animals were listening carefully.

They thought and thought about what
they heard. They thought about the
club. They thought about Springer.
They thought about the courage
Chopsie had used to quit the club.

First, Blossom said,
"I quit the club."

Then, Grinder said,
"I quit the club."

Next, Burly said,
"I quit the club."

Tipper looked around. He was the only member left. He thought, "What good is a club without members?" So he said, "Oh, all right, I quit the club, too. I'll go get Springer and bring him back."

Chopsie said, "I know what we can do. Let's start a new club. Anyone who has the COURAGE to speak up and stand up for his friends can join. I'll be president!"

The Special-Berry Drink

"Meeting at the clubhouse! Let's go!"
said Grinder to Chopsie.

"Fun meeting at the clubhouse! Let's
go!" said Tipper to Springer.

"Big, fun meeting at the clubhouse!
Let's go!" said Sage to Burly.

Blossom was busy getting ready
for the meeting. She loved to invite
her Principle Woods friends to her
clubhouse. She loved to show off. She
loved to tell them about the good
food they would eat.

Today, she had promised them cool,
yummy Special-Berry Drinks. It was a
hot day. They were very thirsty. They
hoped Blossom would hurry up, but,
of course, she did not.

"You stay here," Blossom said in her
bossy, I-am-better-than-you voice.
"Only I know what the secret recipe
is. Only I know how to make Special-
Berry Drinks. Only I know how to
make them the right way."

She disappeared into the clubhouse.
She held her nose and tail high in the
air. She did, indeed, look important.

Tipper looked at everyone and said,
"Let's play the game 'Who Am I?'
I'll go first.

Only I know what the secret recipe is.
Only I know how to make the special
drink. Only I know how to make it the
right way. Now, who am I?"

All the animal friends looked at each other. They did not want to laugh. They did not want to shout out the answer, in case Blossom would hear.

Blossom was busy making Special-Berry Drinks. She took out the honey. She took out the cool water. She took out the secret ingredient – a big, ripe, juicy special-berry. She held that beautiful berry high in the air.

It glittered.

It glowed.

She held that beautiful berry high in the air and sniffed. The smell was sweet.

She held that beautiful berry high in
the air and thought, "This berry would
taste so good. I will taste just a tiny
piece of it."

And she did.

"My, that was very good.
I will taste just a little more."

And she did.

"My, that was very, very good. I will
taste just a little, tiny bit more."

And she did.

And it was all gone!

Now she had a problem.

What would she tell her friends?

They would be mad at her.

They might laugh at her.

Then she had an idea.

"Come here, friends," called Blossom,
"I have bad news to tell you. You will
not get your drinks today."

"Why?" shouted all the animals.

They were very thirsty. They were
upset.

"Because." Blossom stopped talking and started again. "Because." Once again Blossom stopped talking. She just could not tell her friends the truth. Instead, she pointed her finger at Tipper and said, "Tipper snuck into my clubhouse and took the special-berry! Blame him!"

"What?" exclaimed Burly, the big bear.
"That cannot be true. Tipper was with
us playing the game 'Who Am I?'
He is not the reason we don't have
our drink."

Blossom said, "What? Don't you believe me? How dare you tell me Tipper didn't take the berry? I think it's time you all go home. This meeting is over."

The animal friends were sad and slowly walked away.

Blossom was sad, too. The meeting was over because of her. A meeting is not any fun without friends.

Blossom was mad, too. She was mad at herself for not having the COURAGE to tell the truth.

She thought and thought about
what she had done. She thought and
thought about what she had not done.
She thought and thought about how
she could fix what she had done.

Then, she got busy.

First, she sent Springer out to invite all her friends to the clubhouse. The bunny hopped from home to home crying, "Listen to this invitation!

Who: All Principle Woods Friends

What: Important Meeting

When: Today – Noon

Where: Clubhouse

Please, please come!"

When everyone arrived, Blossom said,
"Thank you for coming back. I am
sorry I asked you to leave. I am sorry
that I did not tell the truth. I am the
one who took the special-berry. I ate
it all up. I didn't mean to, but I did. I
thought you would all laugh at me if
I told you. So I said Tipper did it. I am
sorry, Tipper. I did a mean thing to
you. I am so sorry."

Then Sage spoke. "Blossom, I am proud of you for telling the truth. Everyone makes mistakes, but mistakes can always be fixed. You had the courage to fix your mistake today. Now, let's have a party celebrating COURAGE! We can start with a special-berry hunt!"

Recipe for Special-Berry Drink

You will need:

1/2 banana
5 strawberries
or raspberries

1 cup yogurt
2 tsp. honey
ice cubes

1. Cut up banana and put in blender with berries.
2. Add yogurt, honey and 2 or 3 ice cubes.
3. Mix in blender until smooth.